FINDING
HOPE

ReadZone Books Limited
www.ReadZoneBooks.com

© in this edition 2016 ReadZone Books Limited

This print edition published in cooperation with Fiction Express, who first published this title in weekly instalments as an interactive e-book.

FICTI🗨N EXPRESS

Fiction Express
First Floor Office, 2 College Street,
Ludlow, Shropshire SY8 1AN
www.fictionexpress.co.uk

Find out more about Fiction Express on pages 92–93.

Design: Laura Durman & Keith Williams
Cover Image: Bigstock

© in the text 2015 Marie-Louise Jensen
The moral right of the author has been asserted.

ISBN 9-781-78322-582-8

Printed in Malta by Melita Press.

FINDING HOPE

HOPE

Marie-Louise Jensen

What do other readers think?

Here are some comments left on the Fiction Express blog about this book:

"I love the book! Faly's story was so sad. I hope you can make a sequel about Faly."
Francesca, King's Lynn

"We have just read the first chapter of Finding Hope *as a whole class.*

Sasha felt it gave the reader lots of images in your head and you were always wondering what would happen next. Harry said he thought the story was admirable and he also like the cliff hanger at the end [of the chapter] Nicole – "It drew you in and made you wonder about the character."
Nicola Grant and the 6G Literacy Group, Ludlow Junior School

"Wow! Finding Hope *was an amazing story."*
Eman and Moneba, Hertfordshire

"Such a good ending to Finding Hope. *Very emotional, made a 15-year-old boy cry."*
Pedro F, Devon

Contents

Chapter 1

The New Arrival

Faly

It's cold here. Everything's cold: the air, the house, the colours. It's dark and gloomy and I don't like it. And everyone is pale, so pale, as if they never ever see the sun. I shiver.

The woman with the pale face and the yellow hair is talking to me. I don't know what she's saying. I don't understand the sounds. She takes my hand and I flinch. Reluctantly, I let her lead me through a doorway and into a room. The man, with no hair on his shiny head, puts my bag on the floor and talks to me too. Meaningless noise.

I look back at them. I don't know what they want from me. I don't know where I am… why I am here.

The woman is showing me inside the empty wardrobe and drawers. She puts my clothes away. My spare dress, my few t-shirts. There's a sink in the corner of the room. She puts my toothbrush on it. I must be staying here tonight.

I look around. There is only one bed. Where do the others sleep? There are clean towels on the bed. It's a big, clean room. But the walls are an icy pale blue. It's so… *empty*.

The man pulls some things out of a drawer. Brightly coloured boxes. I don't know what they are. But then I see a pad of paper. Some coloured pencils. I look at them.

The man points to them and to me and talks. I don't know what he means. He puts them into my hands and I close my fingers around them.

They both stand, smiling awkwardly at me, then they go. I sit on the soft bed, clutching the pencils in one hand and stroking the sketchbook with the other. I close my eyes.

I remember. A hot day, vibrant with colours, long, long ago. The scent of flowers drifts in through the doorway; big red flowers. I'm so small, I only reach to my mamma's waist. The sun beats down on the dusty ground, but I'm in the shade indoors, drawing the flowers with a red pencil. Every now and then a fly bothers me. I pause to swipe it away. Everything is peaceful; safe. Mamma's cooking at the stove, singing. My sister's studying her school books. Happy… safe… warm.

In the distance, I hear bangs. I look up, dropping my pencil on the floor. The bangs come closer; get louder.

Dadda comes running. "Faly, Ndella!" he shouts. "We have to go!" Mamma is staring, open-mouthed. Then she yanks the pan from the stove and wraps it in a cloth. Dadda grabs my hand. "Run with me!" he shouts. "We all have to run!"

I try to pick up my pencils but I knock them over. The bangs are close by now, shaking the ground. Explosions. I hear screams. I start crying. "My pencils!" I cry. "We'll come back for them!" Dadda promises, as he pulls me outside and into the undergrowth with my mamma and my sister.

But we never do. I never saw pencils again… until now.

I open my eyes. Here I sit in a cold room… by myself… in a strange land. I think it's Europe. Dadda said if we could get to Europe we'd be safe. Maybe I am safe now. But I never expected to be here alone.

I pull one pencil out of the plastic packet and test the lead. It's sharp. A sharp, bright red. I open the sketchbook and make a bold red mark on the paper. I remember the red flowers.

Then I panic. What if I'm not allowed to draw on here? What if it belongs to someone else? I hurriedly close the sketchbook and put it back in the drawer with the pencils.

* * *

Jake

I'm so glad to be back home. We spent a whole

week in Italy sitting around, filling in forms, answering questions, filling in more forms, waiting, waiting…for what? A sister I never asked for.

"Jake, where do you think you're going?" Mum demands, outraged.

I pause, halfway through pulling on my wellies by the back door and look up at her. "Mum, you know I'm trying to train Thunder for next week's show-jumping event," I remind her. "Of course I'm going straight out to see him – get some practice in!"

"What about your new sister?" says Dad, disapproving. "It's rude to rush out and leave her on her first day!"

I look at my new 'sister'. She's standing in the doorway, watching us with big, scared eyes.

"I think Faly will enjoy having you to herself," I say. "To help her…" I was going to say unpack, but stop myself just in time. Faly hardly had any belongings when we collected her. "You know… to… um… settle in!" I say instead. "Please, Mum, I'm so far behind!" I look beseechingly at my mum, who sighs and shrugs.

"Off you go then, Jake," she says. "But don't be late back! Supper's at seven."

England's a whole lot cooler than Italy, so I grab a jacket and make a run for it before Mum can change her mind.

* * *

"Jake!" cries my friend Tegan as I arrive at the riding stables, just a short walk from my house. "You're back! We missed you!" She's carrying a saddle over one arm and a bridle in her free hand. "Matt, Jake's back!" she yells, disappearing into the big tack room at the end of the stable block.

Matt leads a pony out of the indoor riding school and pauses by me. "Awesome," he says. "We need someone to stable the other horses. You up for helping?"

"I was about to go and see Thunder," I object, but just then Jennie, the owner of the stables puts her head out of the riding school. She's neat and tidy even at the end of a long day, her hair in a net under her smart riding hat and her jacket uncreased.

"Give us a hand, will you, Jake?" she says. You can't argue with Jennie, so I go and fetch the horses from the last riding lesson of the day and untack them.

"How's Thunder?" I ask Tegan as she gives me a hand removing their saddles and bridles and rubbing them down.

"He's doing great," says Tegan. "I rode him every day, like you asked me to. In fact, I'm not sure I want to give him back! So, how was Italy?" Tegan asks tentatively. "Did everything go… um… well?"

I shrug. "S'pose," I say.

Tegan brushes the dried mud off one of the horse's legs. "You brought back the girl – what's her name?"

"Faly. Yes, she came with us. My mum and dad still have, like, a ton of paperwork to do though, to get the adoption recognized."

"Wow. So that's pretty exciting, right? To adopt a sister for you like that!

"She's not for me," I retort. "I never asked for her."

"Well I think it's awesome of your parents to rescue a refugee. Why didn't you bring her with you? I can't wait to meet her."

"She only just got here!" I say. "Besides, she's… she's a bit weird.

"What do you mean?" asks Tegan, frowning at me.

"Well, she doesn't… speak," I explain. "At *all*. She hasn't said a word to any of us since we met her last week."

"Wow, OK, that *is* weird," says Tegan.

"No one knows whether she can't speak or if she just doesn't understand English," I continue. "But she's just scared all the time."

"That's understandable, though," says Tegan, "considering what she's been through."

"But that's just it," I say. "No one knows what she's been through… and anyway, she's safe now, with us. There's nothing to be scared of."

"Yeah, but maybe she doesn't know that yet," Tegan points out. "It might take a bit of time."

I nod. I guess I hadn't really thought of that before.

* * *

Thunder whickers happily when I finally go to his loose box. He nuzzles my pocket for carrots. "Here you are, greedy!" I tell him, holding out the carrot. I saddle him up and take him across to the outdoor school.

I put Thunder through his paces: walk, trot, canter and then we do some figures of eight. Once he's warmed up, I take him out into the paddock and put him at some of the easy jumps. He soars over them, making them look simple. When he jumps, I feel as though I'm flying.

"What's your adopted sister like, then?" asks Matt, leaning on the fence, watching.

"Quiet," I say with a grimace.

"How old is she?"

"She's about our age, we think. Maybe a year younger. But she had no papers so we don't know anything about her for sure."

"It must be strange for her coming to England and everything."

"Yeah," I agree. "Yeah, it must be."

"Why don't you bring her to the stables tomorrow?" says Matt. "She'll enjoy meeting the horses."

"Sure," I say. But I don't mean it. This is my world – my friends, my horse. Mum and dad have got this whole thing about adopting a refugee and offering her a home, and that's fine, but I didn't sign up for it. I don't want her tagging after me everywhere. For all I know, she doesn't even like horses.

When we've finished, Jennie is sweeping the yard. "So, how's Thunder?" she asks. "Tegan has done good work with him all week."

"He's going beautifully," I say, sliding down out of the saddle, patting Thunder and praising him. "The showjumping event is next week, so we haven't got much more time to train."

"I don't think it'll be a problem," says Jennie. "I can give you an hour early on Saturday if you like."

"Thanks, Jennie," I say. I pull my phone out of my pocket and panic. I have to be home in twenty minutes or Mum'll kill me, and Thunder still needs grooming and feeding. "Gotta dash," I tell her breathlessly, leading Thunder to his loosebox.

Chapter 2

Introductions

Faly

I don't sleep much in the unfamiliar bed. This is a strange family. They don't hug or sing. They don't laugh or cry. They smile at me a lot, but I'm not sure they really mean it. It's as if they're trying very hard. I wonder how long I'll have to stay here.

Right now, though, as we sit having breakfast in the kitchen, they're arguing, I think. Jake, the boy is scowling at me. He's standing by the door. He wants to go out, but the grown-ups are pointing at me.

I watch and wait.

Then the woman beckons me to the door, and pulls some horrible rubbery boots onto my feet.

She holds a coat out to me and I dutifully push my arms into it. She keeps talking to me and pointing to Jake.

Jake opens the door and steps out. Then he pauses and beckons me. I hesitate. He doesn't look as though he wants me to go with him. I didn't need to understand what they were all saying to know that. I'm trying so hard to be brave, like dadda told me. But tears prick my eyes painfully. I shake my head and stand stubbornly still.

Jake turns to go, without me. Maybe I should follow him. I brush my free hand across my eyes. I don't want to be shut up in the silent house with the smiling man and woman again. I step out of the door into the cold and drizzle.

Jake

So here I am, leading Faly to the Ridgeway Riding Stables with me on Saturday. To be honest, I feel a bit guilty. She knew I didn't want her and was about to cry. Those big dark eyes of hers actually filled up with tears and that made my stomach lurch, so I left. But, when I looked back, there she was, following me.

Jennie is busy in the yard when I arrive, but no one else is around.

"This is Faly," I tell her. "My… my adopted sister."

Jennie offers Faly her hand and Faly looks at it. "It's nice to meet you, Faly," says Jennie, putting her hand in her pocket. "How do you like England?"

"She doesn't speak," I have to explain. I guess I'm going to be saying that a lot.

Faly watches from the paddock fence while I train with Thunder and Jennie coaches me. Afterwards I bring Thunder up to her. "You can stroke him if you want," I tell her and mime it for her. Faly shakes her head, looking frightened.

I lead Thunder back to the yard and Faly follows at a distance. The other workers are bringing the horses in from the paddocks to be groomed and tacked up for the first lessons of the day. Young children are arriving, riding hats on their heads, coming to stroke the horses and finding out which ones they will be riding today.

Matt sees me and Faly and his mouth drops open.

"Is this your…?" he asks.

"My sister… sort of. Yeah," I say awkwardly. The word still feels strange in my mouth. I've been an only child all my life, and suddenly I have a 'sister' from another continent.

Tegan appears. "Is this Faly?" she asks excitedly. I nod.

"Hello Faly," she says. "Welcome to the Ridgeway! Wow, welcome to England." And she gives her a big hug.

An amazing thing happens: Faly smiles. I haven't seen her smile before. It's only a brief smile, but her whole face brightens; and then it's gone again, like the sun going back behind a cloud.

"She doesn't understand you," I tell Tegan.

"Never mind," says Tegan. "We're going to be friends. I'll show you around, Faly," she says. "Come with me!" She takes Faly's hand and the two of them walk off together. Just like that, I'm free to get on. I feel relieved, but also a little… jealous? Is it because Tegan is *my* friend? Or because Faly is *my* sister?

"Come on, Jake!" calls Jennie. "These horses won't get themselves ready you know! First lesson in five minutes!"

Realizing I'm standing gawping, I get back to work. The deal I have at the Ridgeway is that I get grazing and stabling for my horse if I work a full day every weekend at the stables. My parents pay for Thunder's feed and equipment, but I have to promise to keep up with my schoolwork in return. So I'm always busy.

Saturday is my work day and I spend it sorting out horses for eager young riders, checking the tack between each lesson, dealing with problems, and when I have time, doing some mucking out.

At the very end of the afternoon, when we're clearing up, a Land Rover trundles into the yard towing a horsebox.

"Ah, this will be the new horse," says Jennie.

"New horse?" asks Tegan. "That's the first I've heard about it!"

"I thought I'd told you about her. The RSPCA contacted us about rehoming a mistreated horse, and of course, I couldn't say no."

"Oh," cries Tegan, sympathetically. "Look at her, the poor thing! You were quite right! We've got to help her."

But when the horse is backed out of the box, held on a tight rein by two men, one either side, we begin to have our doubts. The horse is a chestnut mare, thin and bony, and covered in sores and mud. Her neck snakes this way and that, her teeth bared, as she tries to bite first one man then the other. She kicks the horsebox and scrabbles her hooves on the ramp, trying to get away. The men are red-faced and sweating by the time the mare has been tied to the grooming rail.

"Oh dear," says Jennie, looking at her new acquisition. "They didn't warn me she was vicious."

The horse is fighting its tether at the rail, stamping and throwing its head about.

"I'm not sure if this was such a good idea after all," says Jennie doubtfully. "We're a riding stables. What if one of the children gets bitten?"

"What's her name?" I ask the men.

"No idea," says one, getting out some paperwork for Jennie to sign. "We rescued her from a tumbledown shed in someone's backyard. The owner wasn't answering questions. Lucifer would be a good name, quite honestly."

"That's just mean!" says Tegan. "Can't you see how neglected she's been?"

"Arr, but she's vicious," replied the man. He rolls up his sleeve to show us two bite marks. "I'd have her destroyed myself," he tells us.

"We'll put her in the paddock on her own overnight," says Jennie, "and see how she settles in."

The men lead the horse away while I help Jennie sweep the yard and lock up. I don't know where Faly has gone, but I hope she's all right.

Faly

I lie in my bed, staring at the white ceiling. I liked the place where the horses were. It smelled of outdoors and animals, like my… like my village. Tegan was nice. She made me feel welcome and showed me around.

Then this new horse arrived and everyone stared at it. It was very wild. I wonder whether it is just scared and lonely… like me. When everyone had gone back to work I went over to the paddock where the wild horse was. They had untied her and she was galloping about the field and shaking her head. Then she saw me. We looked at each other for a long time. She seemed to calm down, just a little.

I turn out the light and try to go to sleep.

Chapter 3

Lost…

The smell of bacon grilling wakes me. It's Sunday morning. I've got the whole day today to train Thunder. Excitedly, I bounce out of bed, tug my clothes on and head down the stairs.

"Morning, Jake," says Mum with smile. "Hungry?"

The bacon is sizzling, the eggs are scrambling in the pan and the bread is toasting. A cooked breakfast is our Sunday morning treat. "Starving!" I tell Mum, pulling a chair out. Dad's getting the plates out and laying the table.

"Jake, please just fetch Faly before you sit down, will you?" asks Mum.

Faly. I'd almost forgotten about her. "Oh," I

say. "All right then. I won't be a second."

I head upstairs and knock on Faly's door. There's no reply. "Faly?" I call. When she still doesn't answer, I open the door a short way and peer into the dark room. The bed is empty.

"She's not in her room," I tell mum as I sit down and drink my orange juice.

Mum drops the wooden spoon she was stirring the beans with and tomato sauce splatters onto the counter. "Not in her room?" she asks, shocked.

"Chill, Mum. She'll be around somewhere, I'm sure," I say with a shrug, loading up my plate with toast, bacon, sausage and egg. I just love Sunday breakfast.

Mum goes upstairs to check Faly's room and the bathroom.

"Don't you believe me?" I ask through a mouthful of scrambled egg.

"Don't talk when you're eating!" says Mum, distractedly. "Faly?" she calls, walking through the house. "Faly, where are you?"

"Her clothes are gone," she tells Dad. "So she got dressed."

"The back door is unlocked," says Dad. "I know I locked up last night. She probably hasn't gone far. You look in the back garden; I'll check the street."

I keep munching my delicious breakfast, quite certain that they'll come back in with Faly any second. But they don't. Mum is pale when she rushes back in and dad is frowning.

"She's taken her boots, too!" Dad says, pointing at the space by the back door.

"Where can she have gone?" cries Mum. "You don't think she's…. Should we call the police?"

"Let's have a thorough search for her first," says Dad, trying to sound reassuring.

"I can't believe you're just sitting there, stuffing your face, Jake!" says Mum. "Help us look for your sister!"

I don't believe it. First I have a new sister I never asked for. Then I have to share my life at the stables with her, and now she's gone off somewhere without telling anyone. My life was perfect, just about, now Faly's messing it up.

"But I'm hungry!" I object. "She can't have gone far. She doesn't know anyone!"

"Jake, she could be in danger! This could be a matter of life or death! You've got to help us find her!" Mum starts wringing her hands and Dad grabs his jacket. I realize they're really worried about Faly, so I get up reluctantly and pull my wellies on. "OK, I'll help," I mumble. "I'll bet I know where she is, anyway."

"You do?" Mum and Dad say, almost together.

"She'll be at the stables. You'll see. Look, you keep searching around here. I'll try there."

My parents head off in different directions, calling Faly's name. I hurry to the stables, eating a last piece of toast as I go. Bother Faly, making all this trouble. She probably just went for a walk.

"Jennie," I say, walking into the yard. "You haven't seen Faly, have you?"

"Faly?" asks Jennie, turning around, looking distracted. "No! It's the new horse I'm worried about!" She strides across the yard to the office, calling to me over her shoulder. "She's escaped! I'm praying she hasn't caused an accident already! Will you call Tegan and go and look for her, Jake? I have to phone the police!"

Great. Now I've got a missing person *and* a missing horse on my hands!

Faly

It's morning. The rain has stopped… finally. Pale sunshine is peeking through a gap between my curtains when I wake up. It's silent in the house. It's not like my village, where it was all hustle bustle as soon as the sun was up. I think about my family, and what happened to us. I lie awake, thinking, thinking:

Thousands of people crammed into a camp with high fences. We're living in tents and huts made of bits of metal, wood and sacking. There's nothing to do and nowhere to go. No school, no work, no fun. We have to queue up for food once a day.

There are flies everywhere. It's hot and dusty.
Sometimes my sister and I play with the other
children, but there's no lake to swim in or trees
to play among like at home.

"At least we're safe here," Dadda says. "Safe from
the war."

We walked for weeks to get here, past burned-
down villages and empty farms, foraging for edible
plants. Sometimes we heard gunshots and hid in
the bush.

"But there's no hope here," says Mamma. "No
future. We can't stay here. This is no place for Faly
and Ndella to grow up!"

No place for us, anywhere.… I start thinking
about that horse which arrived yesterday. The thin
one that was frightened and hurt. She came from
a bad place, too; I wonder how she is today.

I'm wide awake and restless. I want to go and
see the horse right now.

I think I can remember the way to the stables.
It was down at the end of the road and then

along a path. I could find that again easily, couldn't I? Very softly, I put on some clothes and tiptoe downstairs. I pull on my boots, unlock the back door with the key that's hanging on the wall and slip outside.

The boots make a funny noise as I walk. A sort of *wump wump* sound. It's very loud in the stillness of the early morning. As I walk down the path, past bushes and trees, I notice droplets of dew sparkling on the ends of all the leaves, like tiny jewels. I can feel the early morning sun warming my face. There's a fresh smell of earth and grass. Maybe it isn't so bad here, after all.

I'm proud of myself (and a tiny bit relieved) when I find the stables. There's no one here, just lots of horses looking curiously over the open half-doors of their stables. One brown horse neighs at me, making me jump. Perhaps he wants his breakfast.

I cross the yard and head to the paddock where they put the wild horse. I can't see her. I step up onto the gate for a better view, but I still can't see her, so I climb into the paddock. Maybe the horse is just out of sight. I'm halfway across the field when I see a broken and trampled place in the hedge. The horse hasn't just been moved – she's escaped. That's not good at all.

I go back to the yard to find someone. I can't *tell* them what's happened, but I can *show* them. There's no one here at all. The office and the room with the saddles are both locked. It's still too early. I tug open the door to the indoor riding school and peep in, but it's empty. I can't close the door again, so I just leave it ajar. I stand frozen in indecision. What should I do?

Chapter 4

…and Found

Jake

I ring Tegan's number, and she answers, blearily.

"Jake? What's up?" she says.

"You've got to come to the stables," I tell her. "Faly's gone missing! So has the new horse. Can you help us look for them?"

"Do you think they've escaped together?" Tegan asks.

"I hadn't thought of that!" I say, struck by this new idea. "But surely the horse is too wild for Faly to have taken it?"

* * *

In five minutes Tegan's at the stables.

"We think Faly might have taken the horse," she says to Jennie. "She couldn't take her eyes off it yesterday, remember?"

"That's not possible," Jennie replies. The horse has broken through the hedge. If Faly had taken it, she'd have opened the gate, wouldn't she? Anyway, the tack room was still locked."

"Oh," says Tegan. "OK. We'll go and search now."

"Jake!" Jennie calls me back as we're running off. "The door to the riding school was open when I got here. So I suppose Faly might have been here."

"Thanks," I tell her.

"Where would you have gone this morning if you were Faly?" Tegan asks.

"I've no idea," I say. "I was sure she would be here."

I grab a leading rein from the hook in the tack room, just in case, and we head to the broken hedge in the paddock.

"Look, hoofmarks leading down towards the coast," I say, pointing at the churned up ground.

"And bootprints," says Tegan. "Faly must have gone looking for her, too. But it's so dangerous by those cliffs… for both of them."

Faly

Following the horse's trail is easy. Her hoofprints are very visible in the muddy ground. I hurry along for what seems like ages. Finally the path I'm following opens onto a big green space, and there she is, the horse – thin and dirty, but her head is held high, her ears are pricked forwards, and she's sniffing the fresh breeze. She looks beautiful.

I approach her very slowly and cautiously. She swings her head round to watch me and I pause. After a few moments, I walk forward again. The horse stands quite still, just watching me. She's trembling a little. When I reach her, I put a hand gently on her shoulder.

To my amazement, she doesn't jump or run away. She nuzzles me gently, blowing hay-scented breath on me. Then, quite calmly, she drops her head and starts cropping the grass, her

teeth making little tearing noises as she grazes.
I stand beside her, one hand still resting on her
warm hide. The poor, frightened horse. She just
needs some love.

But how am I going to get her back to the
stables?

Jake

We follow the tracks across a field, along a
footpath and across another field until we get to
the big meadow that leads down to the cliffs.
Just ahead, I spot a small figure in wellies.

"Faly!" I shout, recognizing her.

The figure turns round and puts a finger to her
lips. But it's too late. My voice has startled the
new horse, who was beside her. She throws up
her head and gallops off. Faly looks at me
reproachfully. "I'm sorry!" I tell her guiltily.
"I hadn't seen her."

Faly walks over and takes the leading rein out of
my hand. Then she gestures for Tegan and me to
back off and very slowly approaches the horse. To

our amazement, it lets her walk right up to it and stroke it. I stand there, holding my breath, until she clips the rein onto the escaped horse's halter.

"Wow, well done, Faly!" says Tegan quietly, but with a beaming smile. Faly smiles back. She knows we're pleased. Very slowly, she starts walking back towards the stables and with lots of pauses and hesitations, the horse follows her. It's going to take ages to get the horse back to the stables.

"I'm so, so late to start training Thunder today," I say with a sigh. "Oops, just remembered something!" I pull out my phone and hit 'mum' in contacts. "Mum? It's all OK. Faly's here…."

"Were they very worried about her?" asks Tegan as I ring off.

"Yeah. Sunday breakfast even got cancelled!" I say. "They're meeting us in the stables to see for themselves she's all right."

"Ooh, you should ring Jennie too," says Tegan. "Tell her we've found her horse!"

"I can't," I tell her. "I've just run out of battery."

Just then a pheasant flies up out of the hedge ahead with a great flapping and squawking, and the horse spooks, rearing and tearing the leading rein out of Faly's hands. The horse flees back up the path at a fast trot, only stopping once the bird has flown away. We have to calm her all over again; Tegan and I talk soothingly to her while Faly catches her.

"I'm not going to get to train at all today," I say, biting my lip and anxiously wondering how long it will take us to get back.

"Chill, it can't even be lunchtime yet!" says Tegan. "Faly's doing an amazing job of this! Look, we're nearly back. Why don't you run ahead and ask Jennie where she wants us to put the horse?"

"Good idea!" I say eagerly.

"Oh and Jake!" calls Tegan as I head off. "Make sure the yard is nice and quiet so the horse doesn't spook again! Warn us if not, won't you?"

* * *

I run back to the stables and to my horror, I find it swarming with people. Mum and Dad are there with a packet of sandwiches for Faly, Jennie is talking to two policemen and a squad car is parked just outside the gate. One riding lesson has just ended and another is about to begin, so there are kids and horses everywhere.

"Jennie!" I say. "We've got the horse safe! But we need to…!"

"Jake!" cry Mum and Dad, rushing up to me. "Where's Faly? Why did you leave her? Are you sure she's all right!"

"Yes, she's fine! Hang on!" I say, trying to shake them off, but they keep talking.

"Jennie, I really need to explain…." I begin.

"Did you say the horse has been found, young man?" says one of the policeman. "Is it in a dangerous place?"

"It's fine except that we *really* need to clear the yard, because…" I start saying, but then over all the commotion, I hear the clop of hooves approaching and realize it's too late….

Faly

The horse follows me beautifully, and the last bit of the way, she even speeds up. It's all going so well, until we get into the yard of the stables. Then everything happens at once. There are some men there, in black uniforms, talking to Jennie. I look at them, scared, but they don't seem to have guns. The horse starts trembling and her ears go back flat against her head. A door slams.

The poor horse jumps and then rears up and screams in fear, tearing the leading rope through my hands. Then she kicks out, sending a wheelbarrow and a broom flying, and tries to gallop away. Luckily, Jennie quickly closes the yard gate so the horse can't escape. But she neighs and canters around, her head and tail held high. Everyone's running around the yard trying to catch her, which terrifies her. Then Jake jumps on a horse and tries to ride up beside the wild horse to catch her, but it panics her even more.... They're all shouting at me. What can I do?

Chapter 5

Police and Pandemonium

Jake

The whole stable yard has gone mad! People and horses are charging everywhere. The wild mare has upset the other horses and one of them has got loose. A little boy is crying, two girls have jumped over the gate to get away and the policemen are furious. Faly looks terrified. She's standing staring at the scene with wide eyes.

"Someone get that horse under control!" one of the policeman yells.

"If you would get out of my way, Sergeant, I might be able to do so!" Jennie retorts.

The poor wild horse is backed into a corner. I can see she's just frightened, but the parents who are collecting and dropping off their children are complaining in loud voices. Some are even threatening to take their children away from the stables.

I can't bear all the shouting. I carefully climb down from my horse and cross the yard to where Jennie is approaching the mare, talking soothingly. Just as she reaches out to take hold of the lead rein, the sergeant shouts, "Grab her, quick, now!"

The noise frightens the horse and she rears and escapes, barging Jennie out of the way.

Jennie turns, frustrated. "Can you all be quiet?" she orders. "Please! While I *try* to catch this horse."

I try talking to the policemen. "You should let… er… my sister, Faly try…." But the policeman isn't listening.

"This is ridiculous!" he scoffs. "What a lot of fuss about nothing! Leave this to me!"

He strides up behind the horse, just as Jennie is again approaching her head. Bending down, he makes a grab at the lead rein that is trailing across the yard. Seeing the sudden movement behind her and feeling the jerk on the rein, the horse neighs in fear.

"Don't walk behind her…!" cries Jennie. But it's too late.

I watch, frozen with horror, as the horse kicks out hard, catching the policeman on his backside and sending him flying forwards, to land flat on his face in the horse muck that is scattered over the yard.

We all gasp in shock. The horse's hooves clatter across the yard. The sergeant groans and picks himself up. He is clutching himself, wincing in pain and purple with rage.

"That's it! I'm charging you with a whole list of offences!" he snarls at Jennie. "Possession of a dangerous animal! Not keeping said animal under control! Allowing said animal to escape and cause a danger to the public! Wasting police time! Injuring a police officer! Do you want me to continue?"

"Oh, will you be quiet and let me catch this horse?" Jennie snaps.

But she doesn't need to. The trembling horse has fled towards Faly. She's taken her rein and is standing stroking her in the calmest way imaginable.

"Jake!" says Jennie in a hushed voice. "Open the door of that loose box behind you! Well done! Now Faly, lead the horse in – yes, in there!"

Fortunately the policemen have the sense to stay quiet for a few minutes while Faly guides the horse into the box. Once the door is closed, I turn to my sister and say: "Well done!" Then I realize she won't understand me, so I give her a big grin and a thumbs-up. Faly smiles back. It's the first time she's ever smiled at me, and it makes me feel good. Then she looks at my thumbs, lifts her own hands and copies me awkwardly, giving me a thumbs-up back. We both laugh.

Faly

I don't know what Jake is trying to say, but he looks relieved and happy. I'm happy too because he's pleased with me and because the poor horse is safe at last.

Jennie hands me an apple and points to the horse, so I feed it to her. She snatches it from my hand, puts her head in the air and crunches it up. When it's gone, she noses my pockets nervously for more.

Jake's parents come bustling up to us. Jake and his mum talk a lot and they sound cross. I don't know what to make of it. Jake's dad comes over and puts a packet of food in my hand and mimes to me to eat it and when I nod, they turn to go. To my surprise, Jake's mum comes back, gives me a hug and kisses me. She has tears in her eyes. I reach up and touch her cheek gently. I don't want her to be sad. She cries a bit, but she's smiling too now, so I suppose that's better.

When they've gone, Jake and I stroke the mare for a while until she's calm and the yard is quiet again and then Jake goes off to see his own horse.

Standing alone by the wild horse, I can see Jennie in her office talking to the two men in black. I hear one of their voices raised angrily. I shiver. Men in black uniforms frighten me.

I remember. After we leave the camp, we walk for many days. We have no food and nothing much to drink. Finally we reach a place where there are men with guns; men in black clothes. My father pays them a lot of money and in exchange they agree to drive us safely across the desert.

But it isn't safe. Not at all. Mamma says we've been swindled. The lorry is old and rusty and leaks oil onto the sand. It blows clouds of fumes from its rattling exhaust.

We are packed in like animals, with barely any food or water and sent off across the vast desert without a map or a driver who knows the way. Dozens of desperate people fleeing war and hunger.

"This is the Sahara Desert," my dadda tells me as we drive, the heat like a solid wall against us. "One of the hottest places on Earth."

The truck breaks down before we reach the other side. We have no way of fixing it. We walk the rest of the way, those of us who can, struggling through the desert in the blistering heat. I never found out what happened to the ones we left behind. Dadda told me not to worry but…

"Faly?" says Tegan, pulling me out of my thoughts. "Are you okay?" She follows my gaze towards the men in uniforms. She must guess I'm afraid, because she takes my hand and gives it a squeeze.

Jake

I've just saddled Thunder ready to get back to training him – finally – when Matt comes up to me. "Those policemen are insisting the new horse is destroyed," he tells me, a worried frown on his face.

"No way!" I exclaim.

"It's just not right," he says. "I'm going to fetch Tegan. We should talk to them before they go."

"What are they even thinking?" exclaims Tegan indignantly. "She's a rescue horse. She needs a chance!"

"We've got to go and talk to them!" I urge them. "We need to explain. Come on, Faly, we especially need you."

Faly hangs back, but eventually tags along behind us.

When we all file into the office, where Jennie is sitting with the two policemen, I expect her to be annoyed at the interruption. Instead, she greets us with relief.

"Ah, I hoped you join us," she says. "I was just explaining to the officers that you should never, ever walk behind a frightened horse! And also that the horse has only just arrived with us."

"She came from a *very* bad place," explains Matt.

"Where she'd been neglected and treated cruelly," I add.

The police officer looks at us. "Yes, but the animal is clearly dangerous…" he begins.

"No, you don't understand," says Tegan. "She's not vicious; she's frightened. We need time to get her used to us and to feel safe here."

Jennie nods. "Just what I've been saying," she agrees.

The policeman looks unconvinced. "Horses are big animals," he says. "So if they get out of control, they can…"

"We're just going to repair the gap in the hedge now, aren't we, Jennie?" says Matt. "We'll make sure she doesn't escape again."

"Definitely!" Jennie says emphatically. "Never again."

"Also, she's very important to my sister," I say, pulling Faly forward from where she's hiding behind me. "She's bonded with the horse – she's really good at calming it down, as you saw, and she's going to spend a lot of time with her."

"Is that right?" the sergeant asks Faly.

"Faly doesn't speak English yet," explains Tegan quickly. "She's only just…arrived."

"Great, a horse trainer that doesn't speak

any English," groaned the policeman.

I feel frustration boil up inside me. "Faly's a refugee from Africa, and now she's my sister... She's had a bad time, just like the horse. And they're friends, you see. It would break her heart if it had to be… if you took it away."

"All right, all right," says the policeman giving in. "Listen. I'm going to give you one week to get that horse under control. When I come back, I want to be sure the animal is safe to keep here and that it won't escape again. One week! Otherwise I'm going to have to insist it's put to sleep. Agreed?"

"Yes, officer," I say.

They leave at last, the sergeant still limping from being kicked. We all breathe a sigh of relief as they drive off. "A week isn't long to gentle a horse in that state," says Tegan doubtfully.

"We'll have to spend a lot of time with her," says Matt.

"Not me!" I say. "I need to train Thunder!"

"You certainly do," says Jennie, coming back

in from seeing the policemen off. "What are you doing standing around chatting, Jake? We'll take care of the troublesome horse. But first *I* need to go and talk to some angry parents."

Chapter 6

An Angry Outburst

Faly

While Jake goes off with his horse, I help Tegan
and the others carry some posts and planks of wood
from the back of the stable block out to the field.
I know what to do because I used to help grandadda
make pens for his cattle. We dig holes for the posts,
stamp the ground back around them and nail the
planks across the gap where the horse escaped.
Before we let the horse back in, we walk around
the field, checking the rest of the hedge. It seems
safe now. I eat my bag of sandwiches while we're
walking. I hadn't realized how hungry I was.

Back at the stables, Jennie gives me the leading
rein. I understand she wants me to take the horse

back to her field. Tegan and Matt go with me. When I unclip the rein, the horse canters off around the field, head and tail held high. She pauses at the new section of fence, sniffs it and neighs. It's as if she is cross that we've cut off her means of escape. She paws one front hoof on the ground, and then canters off again. We all laugh.

The horse finds the muddiest patch of field, lies down and rolls, wriggling from side to side and waving her legs in the air. When she gets up again, she's got big smears of mud on her and bits of muck and grass stuck in her mane. I think perhaps she's starting to feel more at home now… like me.

Tegan shakes her head and sighs. She talks to Matt while I watch the horse as she sticks her nose in her water trough, takes a long drink and then starts grazing. Tegan sees me staring at them, not knowing what they are saying.

She points at me and says, "Faly". I smile because I know my own name. Then Tegan points to herself and says, "Tegan." I nod, because I already know her name, too.

Then she points at the horse. "Hope!" she says.

She's giving the horse a name. I turn the sound over in my mind. *Hope.* I wonder what it means….

Jake

It's wonderful to finally be riding Thunder. We go for a canter along the downs above the cliffs to get the fidgets out of him. The afternoon sun is shining; the sea breeze is fresh and Thunder strides out beautifully. His fitness is perfect. I pat him and praise him. After about an hour, I turn him back towards the stables and we trot back to the jumping field.

"Right, Thunder," I tell him. "Time to practise for next weekend."

That's when it all goes horribly wrong.

Thunder takes the first jump much too fast and lands hard. "Oof!" I gasp as I'm jolted, "Whoa, Thunder!" But he's racing for the next jump already, I slow him, but he still takes it too fast, knocking the top pole down with a bang. It gives him a fright and he dashes off with the bit between his teeth.

Talking soothingly to him, I rein him in and trot him slowly around the outside of the field to calm him. When I think he's steady again, I put him at another jump, but he refuses, stopping dead in front of it. I go straight over his head. I try to fall as Jennie has taught me, but it still hurts. I think I've twisted my ankle…great!

I'm *very* glad there's no one watching. But the thought that this could happen in the arena next week in front of everyone makes me feel sick.

"Oh, Thunder," I say, giving my horse a pat, once I've got painfully to my feet. "What's up with you?"

I gather the reins, take hold of the pommel, put my uninjured foot into the stirrup and jump into the saddle again. We walk, trot and canter away from the jumps, and that's fine, but as soon as I turn Thunder towards them again, he gets silly. He spooks at the first jump and runs around it, he refuses the second and then crashes straight into the third, scattering the poles all over the ground. It's a complete disaster!

I'm completely humiliated when I realize that Tegan, Matt and Faly are all back from the paddock and standing watching me over the fence.

"What's wrong with you, Jake?" asks Tegan tactlessly. "I haven't seen you ride that badly since you were seven with no front teeth and a runny nose!"

"Everything's wrong!" I snap, angry at her for making fun of me. "I've spent the whole day running around after that stupid wild horse and my stupid 'sister' when I should have been training Thunder! Now I'm injured and he's forgotten how to jump! And instead of winning the event next week, I'm going to come *last*! And I've been looking forward to it for months!"

I turn to Faly. "This is all *your* fault!" I scream. "If you hadn't gone wandering off this morning, none of this would have happened!"

Almost as soon as the words are out of my mouth I'm regretting them. Big tears gather in

Faly's eyes and threaten to spill over. Tegan and Matt both glare at me furiously. But I'm so frustrated, and my ankle is burning with pain. I don't know what to do....

Chapter 7

Making Up

Faly

Jake is sitting high on his horse, yelling words down at me. I don't understand them but I know he's angry; his face is red and twisted. It looks awful. I feel his rage like a hot wave, scalding me.

I turn and run, anywhere, to get away from the anger. Because it reminds me…

Dadda hurries us all to the port. But when he finds the men who have promised to take us to Europe, they push my dadda around and demand more money. "This is only half of what we asked for!" they yell furiously. "We have a good boat, a safe boat; you have to pay properly for it!"

"Give us more money!" shouts the leader, his face twisted up with rage. "We know you have more!"

Dadda shouts, "No!" But the men grab hold of him and rifle through his clothes. "What are you doing?" Dadda yells. "I've paid you what you asked! Get off me!" But the men don't listen. Mamma, Ndella and I stand watching, horrified, too scared to speak.

"What's this?" one of the men jeers, pulling a small roll of hidden notes from my father's pocket. "No," Dadda cries. "You cannot take that. It's the money for our new start in a foreign country." But the leader pockets the money and shoves Dadda away.

We have nothing left but the clothes on our backs. I can feel Dadda's quiet despair as we wait silently at the dockside.

When the boat comes, it's old, leaking and it stinks. So much for good and safe. It's worse than the lorry in the Sahara. I'm frightened to step on, but the men shout at me and push me.

"It'll be all right, Faly," Mamma says, holding my hand tightly as more and more people climb

aboard behind us, cramming the deck until I can
hardly breathe. "Just think," Mamma whispers
soothingly in my ear, "think of the new life we'll
have on the other side of the sea!"

I run to Hope's field, fleeing my memories as
well as Jake's anger, and climb over the gate.
Hope comes trotting towards me, nosing my
pockets for carrots. I get one out and feed it to
her. Then I put my arms around her and hug
her, breathing in her comforting, horsey scent.
She blows air out through her nostrils, and
stands quite still, letting me lean against her.

After a while, Jennie comes to join me. She
smiles at me kindly, strokes the horse, says some
stuff I don't understand and then beckons me to
go with her.

In her office, there's a delicious-looking cake
and she cuts me a piece. I look nervously at it
for a moment, because I'm still upset and
anxious, and I don't want to do anything wrong.
But Jennie mimes eating, puffing her cheeks up

with air and crossing her eyes. She looks so funny, I can't help myself laughing out loud.

Jake

"Look what you've gone and done now!" exclaims Tegan as Faly flees.

"Yeah, well done, mate," adds Matt.

My anger has upset Thunder and he stamps his foot nervously. I slide down out of the saddle, jarring my ankle as I land. I cry out in pain, pull Thunder's reins over his head and lead him to the gate, limping badly. I try to ignore Tegan and Matt, but they follow me as I hobble back to the stable block. "As for *you*," I tell Thunder crossly. "You're a complete disgrace!"

Thunder nudges me with his long nose and snorts softly. "You're not getting round me like that," I tell him, hitching his reins to the grooming rail. But I can't stay angry with him. It was probably my riding that was all wrong, after all.

I'm starting to feel sick. What have I done? The memory of tears in Faly's eyes won't leave me.

"I never asked for a sister," I tell Tegan as I undo Thunder's girth and take his saddle off. Tegan crosses her arms and gives me a death stare.

"She shouldn't have run off this morning," I tell Matt. He shakes his head at me, frowning darkly.

I turn my back on them and start to rub Thunder down, but after a few minutes, I drop the brush and put my head in my hands. "So, I'd better say sorry," I mumble.

"What was that?" asks Tegan. "Didn't quite catch it?"

I turn round. "I'D BETTER SAY SORRY!" I say loudly. "BECAUSE I'M AN IDIOT!"

"You got it," agrees Matt.

"If you can find Faly," says Tegan. "Who knows where she's run off to after you picked on her like that."

* * *

I look for Faly in Hope's field, but she's not there. I look all over the stables and finally find her in Jennie's office. As I open the door and walk in, they're laughing. My first thought is, *Huh! Faly can't have been that upset*. But then she catches sight of me in the doorway. The smile is wiped from her face in an instant and she flinches.

Guilt knots up my insides. I'm not just an idiot, I'm a bully.

"Look, I'm really, *really*, sorry," I say to Faly.

"You know she doesn't understand you," says Jennie. "I overheard you shouting, Jake, and it wasn't pretty."

Shame flushes my face and I stand there with no idea what to do.

"Try getting on your knees," suggests Tegan behind me.

"You've got to be kidding me!" I object.

"Nope," they all say.

So I kneel down in front of Faly and mime praying to her with my hands together. Then I mime crying. Then I mime beating myself up.

I stop when Faly puts a hand on my shoulder. I look up into her face and her lovely dark eyes are calm. I hope that means I'm forgiven.

I want to do something nice for her. So I say the nicest thing I can think of: "Come on, I'll take you for a little ride on Thunder."

Jennie points at Faly and mimes riding, holding the reins. Faly looks apprehensive, but she doesn't shake her head like she has before. So when she's finished her cake, Tegan finds her a hat, Jennie lends her some riding boots and Matt puts Thunder's saddle back on.

I give Faly a leg up. She scrambles awkwardly into the saddle and perches up there, looking terrified. I place her hands on the pommel. "Just hold on," I say. I take the reins and lead Thunder forward. Faly squeaks a little as he moves off.

"Faly must be able to speak," I say to Jennie, who's walking next to me. "Because she has a voice, doesn't she?"

"Sometimes, when children have been through a very traumatic experience," Jennie says, "they lose the ability to speak for a time. You need to be kind and patient with her… and *not* lose your temper."

"I know," I say, ashamed.

Chapter 8

Making Up

Faly

I always thought riding looked easy, but it isn't.
Jake's horse wobbles as he walks. It's bumpy and
jerky and the saddle is slippery to sit on. I cling on
tight and hope it will be over soon. But after a bit,
it stops feeling so bad and I start to enjoy it. Tegan
is smiling and nodding at me and I smile back.

I'm still shaken up by Jake's anger. I still don't
know why he was so mad. But at least he isn't
any more. And I think he was trying to say sorry.

* * *

I spend the next day with Jake's mum. She takes
me shopping for some clothes. I can't believe

she's buying so many things for me. I wonder why? She must be very kind.

Later, when Jake and I have been to the stables, he fetches the paper and pencils from my room. He spreads them out on the kitchen table and starts drawing. I watch him for a bit, then I sit down beside him and draw too. I've wanted to since I got here. Jake draws his horse – the head is too big and the legs look like sticks. We both laugh at it. I draw the red flowers I remember from home; the way they grew around our door.

While I'm colouring in the flowers, Jake fetches some books and pens and starts to write. I finish my drawing and then I look at what he's doing. It's school work, but my heart skips a beat when I look closely.

It's French! Jake is learning a language I know!

Jake

I can tell Faly's excited by my French books, but I don't know why. Then she grabs my exercise

book and scrawls across the bottom *Je suis Faly*.
I know that means 'I am Faly'.

Then I get it. She understands French! But…
I'm confused. I thought she was from Africa.

I call my mum and tell her. Mum is excited,
but not as surprised as me. "They speak French
in lots of African countries, Jake," she explains.
"Senegal and Ivory Coast, for example. Faly
probably speaks an African language, too…
maybe even more than one. The interpreters at
the refugee camp in Italy couldn't work out
which languages Faly knew, because she
wouldn't speak at all."

"Well, this is awesome," I say. "I've got a sister
who can help me with my French homework!"

Faly and I spend the rest of the evening writing
each other simple notes. I don't know much
French yet, just a few words, so it's pretty basic.

One of the last things I write is *Faly, tu es ma
sœur*. You're my sister.

Faly looks up, shocked. Wow. She didn't
know that.

Faly

I can't sleep. I can't get over what Jake told me. This is my new family. I thought I was just staying here, like in the camp or the hostel. But he told me I'm his sister now. His parents are my parents too. That's… so very strange.

Of course it's nice here. They are very kind – most of the time. And I'm getting used to it. But… I miss my own family so much.

Jake

My alarm goes off early in the morning. Switching it off, I suddenly realize it's Saturday, and butterflies swarm into my stomach. It's the day of the showjumping event!

I leap out of bed. Training's been going well since that disastrous session on Sunday last week and I hope today will too. Fortunately, my ankle is feeling much better. I pick up the bag I packed last night containing my smart jodhpurs, jacket and my well-polished boots. Time to go.

It takes hours to load Thunder into the horse box and drive to the event. When we get there, the whole field is buzzing. Competitors are being called over the tannoy, people are warming up their horses and wandering around the traders' stalls.

We all go and look at the ring. The jumps are huge! They look really scary, but an official tells me they'll be lowered for the junior event. Phew!

I warm Thunder up in the practice field. He's jumpy after the ride in the horsebox and silly about being somewhere new. He shies a few times and fusses, but after an hour, he's calmed down and clears the practice jumps well.

"I've got to go," I say, when I hear the junior competitors being called.

"Good luck!" say Mum and Dad. Faly hands me a note she's brought. It says *Bonne chance!*, which I'm guessing is French for 'good luck'.

As I wait in the roped off area for my turn, I can see Faly and my parents watching at the ringside. One by one the juniors ahead of me jump their rounds. One boy falls off, and another horse refuses three jumps so both riders are disqualified. Lots of the competitors have only two or four faults, though. Thunder's going to have to perform really well if we're to be in with a chance.

At long last it's my turn. Thunder trots far too fast into the ring and I have to circle him round to calm him. My hands are shaking with nerves and Thunder can sense it. I take some deep breaths to steady us both and give Thunder a reassuring pat.

The starting bell goes. We canter steadily towards the first jump – a simple vertical. Thunder is pulling on the reins and eager to go. I feel him gather himself as we approach the jump and we're off – soaring through the air and landing neatly on the far side. "Well done, boy!" I praise Thunder as I turn him towards the next two jumps which are close together: an oxer and a hogsback. He jumps these perfectly and I start to relax and enjoy myself. The rest of the course goes smoothly and finally we canter proudly back out of the ring.

We make it through to the final round. "Clear and fast, Thunder," I tell my horse as we ride out into the ring for the second time. But he doesn't need telling. It's as though last weekend never happened. He's a real competitor and wants to win. It feels as if we're flying and I forget the rest of the world exists. It's just me, Thunder and the jumps.

Faly

Jake jumps so well. It looks as though he and his horse are thinking and moving together all the time. His name is up on the big board in lights with just three others.

I watch him complete his round and ride out of the ring. I don't know if he's won, because I don't understand the rules. But Thunder didn't knock down any of the poles like some of the others, so I guess that's good.

Someone taps me on the shoulder. I jump and look round. Two men are standing behind me, staring at me. My heart skips a beat. What do they want with me?

They're talking to me, but I don't understand. I look around wildly for Jake's parents. Over there! I hadn't realized how far I'd strayed, trying to get a good view of Jake. I turn and make a dash back to them, but before I've taken two steps the men grab me!

Jake

I'm fizzing with excitement as the finalists are called back into the ring. Did we jump fast enough to win? Suddenly the tannoy fizzes into life. The booming voice announces, "And the winner is – Jake Williams on Thunder!"

The crowd cheers and claps. I nearly burst with pride as a big blue 1st rosette is pinned onto Thunder's bridle.

As we canter a slow lap of honour around the ring, I wave to Mum and Dad and look for Faly. She's nowhere to be seen. I scan the ringside and that's when I spot her. Two men are dragging

Faly towards a black van. She's struggling like crazy. Then they bundle her inside.

The men jump into the front seats and the van starts to pull away. What's going on?

Chapter 9

Kidnap!

Jake

Panic sears me when I see the black van driving off with my sister captive inside.

Without stopping to think, I turn Thunder away from the victory line. We dash out of the ring and canter swiftly after the van. People jump out of our way as we tear across the grounds, but the van is going faster than we are. I'm hoping against hope that it will get held up at the gate on the way out of the showground and Thunder and I can catch up.

I can see the van slowing ahead. Thunder senses my urgency and lengthens his stride. We're gaining on them, closer, closer….

But then the gate swings slowly open, and the van is through it and onto the road. *Now* what do I do? I can't let them take Faly!

I try and remember the route we took to the ground. We drove down a tiny lane that wound through farmland for several miles.

"I know!" I say aloud. Thunder pricks up his ears. "Are you ready to take a shortcut?" I ask him. Responding to my hand on the reins, Thunder wheels round and heads swiftly across the showground to another gate I spotted earlier. Fortunately, I can reach down from my horse and release the latch. Then we're off, galloping across a huge meadow as the gate swings shut behind us. The wind rushes in my ears and the blue rosette flutters wildly on Thunder's bridle. All I can think about is how terrified Faly must be. Who has snatched her and why?

We pound up over a rise and I see the road winding ahead of us. The van is on it and at first I feel sick at the sight of how far away it is. But then I spot something else – just ahead of the van is a tractor with a huge trailer, trundling along at a snail's pace.

"We can do this! Go, Thunder!" I cry, urging him forward. There's a hedge ahead of us, but it isn't any bigger than the oxer we jumped in the ring, so I head Thunder straight for it. Thunder takes a great leap. I lean forward in the saddle and fly through the air with him. My valiant horse stumbles slightly in the soft soil, but then gathers himself and takes the next field at a canter. As we reach the lane on the far side, I can hear the roar of the tractor approaching. I hope the van is still stuck behind it! I fumble frantically with the rusty bolt on the gate, finally freeing it. We ride right into the middle of the lane, and stop. The farmer slows the tractor to a halt. The van is still behind and my heart leaps with relief.

I haven't thought ahead as to what I'll do when I catch the van. Will two kidnappers hand over their victim just because a boy tells them to? My heart is thumping in my chest with fear, but I *have* to face them. I can't let them steal Faly away.

As Thunder edges past the tractor, the farmer leans out and says, "Hey, what's going on?"

"The men in this van have kidnapped my sister!" I tell him.

The driver of the van looks impatient about the delay, but not the least bit frightened as I approach. The passenger even rolls down the window to speak to me. "What's the hold-up, son?" he asks me.

"Let Faly go!" I order him. "How dare you kidnap my sister?"

"Kidnapping! You're out of your mind, boy," says the van driver, suddenly annoyed. "Get out of our way. NOW!"

"Faly!" I shout, hoping she's unharmed. "Faly, are you in there? Are you okay?"

There's a sudden banging on the van as though someone's trying to kick their way out.

Faly

Despite struggling and fighting with the men, I'm trapped in the back of this van. I don't know what to do. Who are these people and what do they want with me? If only I hadn't wandered off! But I thought I was finally safe here. I think about Jake and his mum and dad and what they will think when they find me gone. Tears come to my eyes. They've been so kind to me. I want to be back with them more than anything.

The van slows and rattles to a halt. I tug at the handle of the van door, but it's locked tight. Then – a miracle! I can hear Jake's voice calling my name! I thump my fists on the side of the van. I *have* to let him know I'm in here.

Jake

The most amazing thing happens. From inside the van comes a voice I don't know: "Jake!" it cries. "*Au secours! C'est moi!*"

It must be Faly! She's calling for help. She's found her voice!

"Let her out!" I yell at the men. "Let her out this second!"

Thunder, sensing my anger, is magnificent. He rears up, right over the van, pawing his front legs in the air and neighing loudly. I cling on tight.

"Here, get that wild beast away from my van!" yells the driver, cowering.

The farmer has switched off the engine of his tractor now and climbed down from his cab. "What's all this about a kidnapping?" he demands.

Behind the van, a Land Rover with a horse box pulls up and hoots impatiently. The kidnappers are trapped!

Once Thunder has all four hooves on the ground again, the passenger gets out of the van with a clipboard. "There's been a misunderstanding, young man," he tells me. "My colleague and I haven't kidnapped anyone." He flashes an ID at me. "We're from the Home Office. We've picked up an illegal immigrant by the name of…" he looks closely at his papers, "Anulika Chukwu."

"No, you haven't!" I cry indignantly. "You took my sister Faly Williams!"

As if to confirm my words, Faly hammers on the side of the van and shouts "Jake!"

"You can't go around snatching people!" says the farmer. "How do you know you've got the right girl?"

"We're just doing our duty!" says the Immigration Officer. "Some illegal immigrants have escaped from a detention centre near here. We had a tip-off from the local police. And we had this…." He shows us a blurry picture of a girl who looks only vaguely like Faly.

"That could be anyone," the farmer exclaims.

The driver of the Land Rover has joined us to see what's going on. "Well, let's see if she *is* his sister!" she suggests.

The Immigration Officer reluctantly unlocks the back of the van and

Faly leaps out. I jump down from Thunder and hug her. "Oh, Faly!" I exclaim, shaking with relief.

"He don't *look* like her brother," says the farmer dubiously, gazing at us standing side by side.

"She's adopted," I tell him. "Legally."

"Ah. That'd explain it," he says.

"Well, I'll need to get confirmation from your parents," says the Immigration Officer.

"No problem," says Jake. "I'll lead the way…."

* * *

I ride back into the showground with Faly up behind me in the saddle. The two Immigration Officers follow in the van. My parents rush over, relieved to see us both. We explain, my mum makes an appointment to show them the adoption papers and everything gets sorted out.

I watch Faly standing, still shocked, as my parents speak to the officials. I try to imagine what it must have been like to be snatched and locked away in a van – especially after everything else she's been through. I suddenly realize how vulnerable she is. She can't even understand what's happening right now.

Chapter 10

Hope Restored

Faly

I can't believe Jake rescued me like that! He's a hero. Every time I think of him and Thunder, galloping after me, I smile. Even though he was so unkind to me the other day, he must care about me to chase all that way. Jake's parents hugged me until I could hardly breathe when they heard what had happened.

Whatever it was that was blocking my voice has gone – as though a great weight has been lifted off me. Now I can't stop talking, just chattering and telling them everything, even though none of them understands me – or not much anyway. Still, it feels so good to finally speak.

When we get home and we've settled Thunder and rewarded him with oats, we all have dinner together and then Jake shows me his rope swing in the garden. It's tied to a tree branch with a big knot in it and you can swing right out over a stream. We take it in turns to swing until Tegan comes round to see how the show went. She gets me to say her name and Jake's… then loads of other things. They both laugh and clap when I try to say their words. Tegan's French is better than Jake's and we actually manage to have a little chat.

Jake

The next morning, I can't wait to take Faly to the stables to show Matt and Jennie that she can talk now.

Jennie wants to know how yesterday's showjumping event went. She is amazed when I tell her the story about Faly's 'kidnap' and rescue. "It sounds as though you could do with a break! Why don't you all take some of the horses down to the beach?" she suggests.

I persuade Faly to come with us on a quiet horse called Toffee. I put a leading rein on him, so she doesn't have to do anything except hold on. I keep an eye on her and she's fine riding along the path and she seems happy on the beach too. We trot and canter the horses along the sand and then slow to let the horses walk in the shallow surf, because the salt water is good for their legs.

We're all having fun when out of the blue, two dogs rush up to us, barking madly. Toffee, who's nearest, shies, and poor Faly falls off into the water.

Faly

The horse swerves so fast, I lose my grip and tumble into the water.

Just as I fall, a wave washes into my face. I gasp and choke. I feel as if I'm drowning again.

We're far out to sea with no drinking water left. The boat is leaking. Everyone on board takes it in turns to bail out the water, but it's coming in faster and faster. Then a wind blows up. The sea becomes choppy and there's water splashing over the sides too. We're all frightened. My dadda is holding my hand and my mamma is hugging Ndella tight.

"It's OK, Faly," says Dadda joyfully. "Look! We're going to be rescued!"

I look in the direction he's pointing and it's true, there are several big boats coming towards us! Everyone runs to one side of our boat waving and calling in excitement, but then a terrible thing happens – the boat tips right over.

So many people are in the water, splashing and calling out. I can swim, but others cannot. The waves are big, and we are all struggling. I can't see my family, but other people are being rescued. All around us, the kind people on the large boats are pulling us out of the water.

On board the rescue boat, I'm given a blanket and a cup of something sweet to drink. The crew are looking after us all, making sure we're not hurt. But where are my family?

"Faly! Faly, it's ok, you're safe!" someone is saying. For a moment, I think it's my mamma, but then I realize it's Tegan. She's helping me out of the waves. We're sitting on the beach. Her arm is around me. Jake and Matt are there too. They look concerned.

I take a deep shaky breath and hold onto Tegan tightly. That was a bad memory. Most of the time, I push that one away. But here I am, safe on the dry sand with Jake, Tegan and Matt. The horses are waiting patiently.

"*Ça va*," I tell them with a nod. I'm OK.

Jake

Something really frightened Faly. It was more than just a tumble into shallow water; because that can't have hurt her at all. But she bravely remounts Toffee and we head to the stables. As we're riding back, I remember something my parents told me. I didn't pay that much attention at the time, but they said the only thing we knew about Faly was that she was rescued from the sea. She nearly drowned. That's why falling in just now scared her so much….

When we get back, I attempt to cheer Faly up by taking her to see Hope. The mare has filled out a lot in the week she's been with us. Her sores have started healing and her coat is looking glossier. She nickers happily when she sees us and comes trotting over, but it's Faly she goes to. Faly feeds her a carrot and makes a fuss of her, speaking to her in French. Then she takes the lead rein from my hand and clips it onto Hope's halter. We watch as Faly climbs over the fence and begins to lead Hope calmly around the enclosure. The horse trots obediently behind her and Faly grins as she circles back to us.

"She's doing well, isn't she?" says Matt.

"It's the name that did it," says Tegan. "Hope."

"'Ope," Faly tries to imitate her.

"H," says Tegan helpfully. "H..H..H..Hope!"

"'Ope," repeats Faly. We all grin.

A thought strikes me. "It means '*espoir*'," I translate for her. I can see she gets it straight away.

"Ah, *espoir*!" she says.

"Fingers crossed she really does have hope," says Matt, patting the horse's neck. "That policeman's coming today to make a decision about her."

"Don't remind me!" says Tegan with a shudder.

"I have good news!" says Jennie behind us. We all turn around to see the policeman standing next to her. He's looking much friendlier than the last time we saw him.

"Sergeant Smith has just spent the last ten minutes watching you all and has agreed that Hope can remain with us," Jennie tells us. She gives us all a big smile and a wink.

"Yes, and perhaps I should come for some training around horses," says the sergeant. "I don't want another hoof up the backside."

He laughs, and we all join in.

As we celebrate the good news, Faly looks on puzzled. I realize she wasn't aware of the danger Hope was in. I'm so relieved that her beloved horse is safe now – Faly already has more than enough to cope with.

"Come back to the office and celebrate with a glass of lemonade," suggests Jennie. "We need to toast Jake for winning his rosette too… and for his heroic rescue of course!"

We turn to follow Jennie. I've just started telling Matt about my winning round at the showjumping event, when I notice Faly has stayed behind with the horse.

Faly

I can understand why they called this poor horse *Espoir*, 'Hope'. She was so hurt and frightened when she arrived. But now she's so much happier. Despite her bad memories, she's found a kind home and someone to look after her… just like me.

I like to think my family were picked up by a different boat that day ours tipped over. Perhaps they were taken to a different place. I hope they're being cared for by kind people, too. Maybe they'll come looking for me. One day, they'll knock on the door and be there, big smiles on their faces. That would be wonderful.

But meanwhile, like Hope, I have a new home. I'm so lucky. I'm getting used to it now and I know I'm going to be happy here. It's just what my parents wanted for me: a better life.

"Faly!" Jake calls. I look round and he's beckoning me. "Lemonade!" he says and mimes drinking. Tegan and Matt are there waiting for me too. I give Hope a goodbye pat, unclip the rein and run to my friends. When I catch up with them, Jake slings an arm around my shoulders and we all walk into the stable yard together.

THE END

FICTION EXPRESS

THE READERS TAKE CONTROL!

Have you ever wanted to change the course of a plot, change a character's destiny, tell an author what to write next?

Well, now you can!

'Finding Hope' was originally written for the award-winning interactive e-book website Fiction Express.

Fiction Express e-books are published in gripping weekly episodes. At the end of each episode, readers are given voting options to decide where the plot goes next. They vote online and the winning vote is then conveyed to the author who writes the next episode, in real time, according to the readers' most popular choice.

www.fictionexpress.co.uk

WINNER
Education Resources
Award for Innovation

FICTION EXPRESS

TALK TO THE AUTHORS

The Fiction Express website features a blog where readers can interact with the authors while they are writing. An exciting and unique opportunity!

FANTASTIC TEACHER RESOURCES

Each weekly Fiction Express episode comes with a PDF of teacher resources packed with ideas to extend the text.

"The teaching resources are fab and easily fill a whole week of literacy lessons!"
Rachel Humphries, teacher at Westacre Middle School

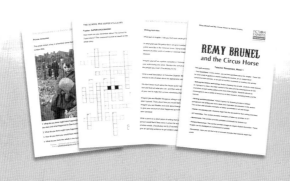

FICTI⬤N EXPRESS

Drama Club
by Marie-Louise Jensen

A group of friends are involved in their local youth drama club at a small city theatre. When their leader, the charismatic Mr Beaven, announces he wants to put on a major new play at the end of the summer holidays, the cast is very excited. Amidst rivalry, hopes and disappointments, will there be more drama on or off the stage? And who will get the leading roles?

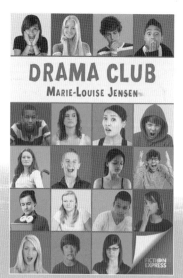

ISBN 978-1-78322-569-9

About the Author

Marie-Louise Jensen was born in Oxfordshire and has an English father and Danish mother. Her early years were largely devoted to the reading of as many books as possible, but also plagued by teachers who wanted her to spend time on less useful things (such as long division).

Marie-Louise studied Danish and German at university and has lived and worked in Denmark and Germany as well as England. She stopped full-time work to home-educate her two sons.

Since 2008 Marie-Louise has had six teen books published by Oxford University Press. She lives in Bath with her two sons and as well as reading and writing teen books and visiting schools, she also enjoys walking, swimming, going to the cinema and travelling.